AH-CHOO

by MERCER MAYER

The Dial Press · New York

To dear friends:
Steve, Helen, and the whole brood
of Kelloggs

Copyright © 1976 by Mercer Mayer · All rights reserved
First Printing · Printed in the United States of America
Library of Congress Cataloging in Publication Data
Mayer, Mercer, 1943—   Ah-choo.
[1. Stories without words] I. Title.
PZ7.M462Ah   [E]   75-9205
ISBN 0-8037-4894-9   ISBN 0-8037-4895-7 lib. bdg.

DATE DUE